ISBN: 978-1-7340616-0-4 (Paperback)
ISBN: 978-1-7340616-1-1 (Ebook)

Illustrations by Denise Glova
Book Design by Mavis O.

D1429846

On a late, cold,
February night, six
collie puppies were born.
Five girls and
one boy.

Oh!
What a joy!

In only a few weeks,
the girls grew big and strong.
So beautiful they were!
Golden like the sun.

Always
jumping and playing!
Pulling and rolling!

The boy was smaller and not so courageous, a little bit shy, a little bit clumsy. His coat was dark and thick but Oh! So shiny!
He felt so different from his sisters.

He liked to sit alone in a corner,
watching them play.

The girls would run to him and ask
him to come and play, but he didn't
have the courage to
join in their game.

His mom would encourage him to play.
She'd push him gently with her long,
slender nose, but he always turned
back,
getting ever closer to her.

Then,
one morning,
Mom said,
"Spring is finally here!
Today,
you can
all go and
explore the
garden."

So many new smells
and things to discover:

Green Grass and
Beautiful Flowers...
Butterflies that whizzed
past their noses!
Birds that sang songs
that they didn't know ...
Even two rabbits hopped around
the beautiful garden!

The girls ran in circles
and barked with joy.

He tried to join in the game,
but the girls would tease him about
being slow and not being able to
keep up with them.

He fell and tumbled.
His coat got dirty
and his paws muddy.
They all started laughing!

So, he went and sat under the blooming tree, trying to hide between the flowers.

The rabbit came over and asked him, "What's the matter?"

He said, "They can run so fast and I can't keep up. I fell and got muddy, and I don't like that."

"Who said that you have to be just like them? You can go at your own pace and still have lots of fun!" the rabbit said.

Each day, they got to play in the garden. The girls ran faster and faster. But, still, he sat alone under the tree smelling the flowers.

Then, one morning, some visitors stopped by. They were all smiles, and the girls were excited to meet them.

He sat under his tree watching the fuss over his sisters. "Oh, how beautiful you are! Oh, how sweet, how cute, how fluffy you are!"

And they truly were!

All five of them were golden like the sun...with white elegant manes and paws. They were perfect little bundles of fur-fluff.

"What's happening?" he asked the rabbit, "Do you know?"

"Yes," the rabbit answered. "They are ready for their new homes, ready to start their new lives."

New home?
New Life?

He got so scared that he hid
underneath
the blooming tree!

When his mother found him, she kissed him with love and encouraged him to come.. "The girls are gone. But, don't worry my son," she said.

"They all went to start their new adventures in loving homes. One day, you will be ready too."

But, he wasn't ready at all.
He still felt frightened. She was a
great mom. Keeping him close for now,
knowing very well that day would come.

He spent day after day lying in the sun,
with the rabbit by his side and his mom
watching him with love.

Then, one morning, he heard
a new voice.
His little heart stopped, and
immediately knew.

Someone had come for him.

"She came for me!"
he said to the rabbit while
he ran as fast as he could to hide
under his tree.
"Then go and say Hi! She seems
very nice."
the rabbit encouraged him.

He looked up from between the flowers and saw her. She had dark hair just like him and a really big smile. She called him to come.

The rabbit said, "Go!"

His mom said, "Don't be afraid! You'll love her in no time!"

He looked at her again. Suddenly, a strange feeling came over him.

He ran! He ran! He ran to her as
fast as he could, and she picked
him up and he just knew.
It was a perfect match!
He felt safe and loved.

"Oh, how cute you are, how fluffy you are! But even more, I heard you were always polite and well mannered. So, I will call you URFY my little gentleman.."

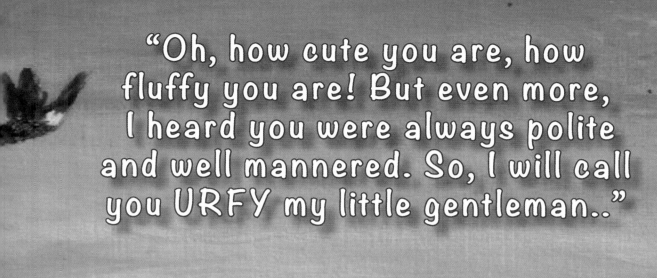

Urfy is a
derivation from
the Hungarian word
Úrfi which means
Little Gentleman.

He loved his name.
He wagged his tail and kissed
her nose. Finally, he was ready
to go to
his new home.

Flora Scheck grew up in Romania, where she was surrounded by nature's beautiful scenery. As a child, she always had a collie by her side. She wrote the "Urfy" series to inspire young children to be sensitive to the purity of the nature around them. Urfy's journey's are thrilling adventures full of joy, wonder, and, most of all, love.

Flora currently resides in Bedminster, NJ with her beloved tricolor collie and a rescue cat who bosses everyone around.

Made in the USA
Monee, IL
07 March 2020